JAM-BO, LITTA-GIRL, AND THE BULLIES

WORDS AND COLORATIONS BY
ADAM B. FORD

LINE-ART ILLUSTRATIONS BY
COURTNEY HUDDLESTON

h bar
press

H BAR PRESS
PHILADELPHIA, PA
WALLINGFORD, VT
2013

To THE
LANDA FAMILY

Adam

Printed in the U.S.A.

First Printing

The typefaces used in this book are PiekosFX Basic and Silverage,
both available from Blambot Comic Fonts and Lettering – blambot.com.

Publisher's Cataloging-in-Publication Data

Ford, Adam B.

Jam-Bo, Litta-Girl, and the Bullies / Adam B. Ford ;
illustrations by Courtney Huddleston.

p. cm.

ISBN: 978-0-9794104-9-9 (pbk.)

1. Bullying--Juvenile fiction. 2. Vocabulary--Fiction.
3. Self-confidence--Fiction.   I. Huddleston, Courtney, ill. II. Title.

PZ7.F75232 Ja 2013

[Fic]--dc23

Library of Congress Control Number: 2013912206

"I LOVE THE POWER OF WORDS,
NOUNS AND VERBS..."

-JURASSIC 5

ON MONDAY, A BULLY NAMED ED BLOCKED MY WAY, AND THEN I WAS LATE FOR MY FIRST CLASS THAT DAY.

ON TUESDAY A BULLY NAMED AL TOOK MY LUNCH.
WHEN I ASKED FOR IT BACK,

HE REPLIED WITH A PUNCH.

ON WEDNESDAY, A BULLY NAMED LU GAVE A PUSH,

AND BOTH LIZA AND I WOUND UP STUCK IN A BUSH.

ON THURSDAY, THE BULLIES ALL SPENT THE WHOLE DAY

TRIPPING BOTH OF US UP

AS WE WENT ON OUR WAY.

THEN ON FRIDAY, THIS MORNING,
THE BULLIES DECLARED:

"WE WILL BEAT
YOU BOTH UP,

SO YOU'D BETTER
BE SCARED."

"ON THE PLAYGROUND AT 3, AFTER SCHOOL,"
GROWLED ED.

AND THEN AL ADDED **"YEAH"**
WHILE LU NODDED HER HEAD.

IT WAS QUARTER TO 3 AND I SAT IN MY CHAIR.
I WAS WAITING, JUST WAITING, TO GET OUT OF THERE.

THEN THE TEACHER SAID,

*"JAMES, IT'S THE END OF THE DAY.
SCHOOL IS OVER, NOW PLEASE,
WON'T YOU GO ON YOUR WAY?"*

I GLANCED OUT THE WINDOW AND THERE BY THE SLIDE
WERE THE BULLIES, ALL THREE,
          LOOKING MEAN, SIDE BY SIDE.

THEN I SAW SOMETHING ELSE,
          AND I MADE A SMALL GROAN.
THERE WAS LIZA IN FRONT OF THOSE BULLIES, ALONE.

WELL, I HAD TO ACT NOW,
  TO SIT STILL WOULD BE CRUEL.

SO I JUMPED FROM MY SEAT
  AND RAN OUT OF THE SCHOOL.

I GOT TO THE SLIDE,
WHERE THE
  BULLIES ALL
    STOOD.

THEY BEGAN TO SURROUND US. THIS WASN'T GOOD.

BUT THEY SAY YOU GET BRAVE
            WHEN THERE'S NOWHERE TO GO.
SO I STOOD TALL AND YELLED AT THEM...

"I AM JAM-BO!"

WITH A LEAP, I JOINED LITTA-GIRL ON THE BENCH THERE
AND WE BOTH FACED THOSE BULLIES,
AND WE GAVE THEM A STARE.

SO WE'RE SMALL,
AND WE'RE QUIET,

AND YOU THINK
THAT WE'RE
NERDS...

BUT WE'LL TAKE
YOU ALL ON

WITH THE POWER OF **WORDS!**

THE BULLIES JUST STOOD THERE,
THEIR JAWS HANGING LOW.

THEN ONE OF THEM STEPPED UP AND SAID TO US,

THAT WAS ALL THAT HE SAID,

JUST THAT 2-LETTER WORD.

AND TO US,
    WELL,

A 2-LETTER WORD'S QUITE ABSURD!

SO WE GOT OURSELVES READY,
WE STOOD TALL AND PROUD,

AND I LOOKED AT THOSE BULLIES
AND SHOUTED OUT LOUD...

"*I AM THE BEST!*"

THAT'S

1, 2, 3, 4.

AND IF THAT'S NOT ENOUGH,
I CAN GIVE YOU SOME MORE...

LIKE **SUPER,** AND **FUNNY,** AND

BRAVE, GREAT, AND **SMART.**

THOSE ARE ALL WORDS WITH **5,**

AND THAT'S JUST A START.

I'M AN **EXPERT,** AND **KINGLY,** **HEROIC,** AND **FASTER.**

I'M **DECENT,** AND **FAMOUS,** A **WIZARD,** A **MASTER!**

WE'RE **MIGHTY** AND **GIFTED** AND **BRAINY** AND **CLEVER.**

ARE WE STOPPING AT **6?** NO, NOT US! NO, NOT EVER!

WE'RE FLOWING WELL NOW,
BUT LET'S ADD ONE MORE LETTER.

WITH **7** WE KNOW THAT WE'LL EVEN DO BETTER!

FOR WE'RE **AWESOME** AND **STELLAR,**

WITH **COPIOUS** TALENT

WE'RE **SPECIAL,**
TITANIC,

SKILLED,
CAPABLE,
GALLANT!

7 WAS HEAVEN, BUT WHAT WOULD BE GREAT,
IS TO ADD ONE MORE LETTER AND GO UP TO **8!**

"WE ARE **DOMINANT, SKILLFUL, SUPERIOR** TOO,

AND **FABULOUS, TALENTED,**

SPLENDID, IT'S TRUE!

WE'RE **SCHOOLED, EDUCATED, TERRIFIC, COMPLETE.**

WE'RE JUST SO **MAJESTIC** THAT WE CAN'T BE BEAT.

"HEY JAM-BO," SAID LITTA-GIRL, "DON'T MAKE A FUSS, BUT HOW 'BOUT SOME **9**S?"

AND I SAID,

"MARVELOUS!"

THAT'S

FANTASTIC,

UPLIFTING,

A

BEAUTIFUL THOUGHT.

WITH OUR

UNEQUALED, MASTERFUL WORD-SKILLS,

WHY NOT?

THESE BULLIES ARE TAKING A **WALLOPING** NOW,
BUT BY USING **10** LETTERS,
ALL OUR WORDS WILL GO

POW!

"STAGGERING!"
LITTA-GIRL SAID,
"AND **STUPENDOUS!**
NOTEWORTHY,
CONSUMMATE,
ALSO
TREMENDOUS!"

AN **EXPERIENCED** MOVE TO ADD ONE TO THE LAST

AND GO FOR *11...* WE'LL BE **UNSURPASSED!**

"**OUTSTANDING!**" I SHOUTED, AND "**EXCEPTIONAL!**" WITH BIG WORDS LIKE THESE, IT WILL NEVER BE DULL.

WE'RE **MAGNIFICENT, CRACKERJACK,** SU-PER-LA-TIVE,

ILLUSTRIOUS, SENSATIONAL, THAT'S HOW WE LIVE."

BUT WAIT! HERE'S SOME **12**-LETTER WORDS
WE CAN BUILD...

ACCOMPLISHED,

CONSIDERABLE,

AND

**MULTI-
SKILLED.**

WE'RE QUITE
ASTRONOMICAL, UNPARALLELED,

WITH
PRIZEWINNING, GREATHEARTED

WORDS THAT WE'VE SPELLED

12? INCOMPARABLE.
13? DISTINGUISHED!

OUR WORDS HAVE DONE MORE THAN WE EVER HAD WISHED.

FOR YOU MIGHT HAVE THE STRENGTH TO COMPLETELY UPEND US,

BUT WE'RE **KNOWLEDGEABLE** AND OUR WORDS WILL DEFEND US.

14!

I SAID, WITH

EXPRESSIVENESS

15!

SAID LITTA-GIRL,

RESOURCEFULNESS!

16.

ENTHUSIASTICALLY

KEEN...

QUITE

INDISTINGUISHABLE

FROM

17.

PHENOMENO-LOGICALLY,

18'S A MESS.

IT'S NOTHING LIKE 19'S

STRAIGHT-FORWARDNESS.

"AND THAT'S IT!"
I PROCLAIMED TO THE BULLIES,
"WE'RE THROUGH!"
YOU DON'T SCARE US AT ALL,
'CAUSE WE'RE SMARTER THAN YOU.

AND WITH THAT WE BOTH TURNED

AND WE JUST WALKED AWAY.

AND THOSE THREE LITTLE BULLIES

HAD NOTHING TO SAY.

1. **I** — A PRONOUN, which takes the place of your name.

2. **AM** — The present tense form of the verb "TO BE".

3. **THE** — With A, and AN, these are ARTICLES.

4. **BEST** — "Best" can be a noun, an adjective, an adverb, or a verb. In this case, it's a noun.

5. **SUPER**
   FUNNY
   BRAVE
   GREAT
   SMART — These are all adjectives. "Super" and "great" are SYNONYMS.

6. **EXPERT**
   KINGLY
   HEROIC
   FASTER
   DECENT
   FAMOUS
   WIZARD
   MASTER
   MIGHTY
   GIFTED
   BRAINY
   CLEVER — The endings "ly" and "ic" mean "like". So KINGLY means "like a king" and HEROIC means "like a hero."

   The ending "er" can sometimes be a COMPARATIVE of an adjective. FASTER is the comparative form of FAST. The SUPERLATIVE of FAST is FASTEST. But "er" is not a comparative in the words MASTER or CLEVER.

**7. AWESOME
STELLAR
COPIOUS
SPECIAL
TITANIC
SKILLED
CAPABLE
GALLANT**

If something is STELLAR it means that it is like a star. It has come to mean anything great or super, shining like a star.

COPIOUS means "a lot." So if you have copious talent, you have tons of talent.

TITANIC means "like a Titan." The Titans were huge giants of Greek mythology.

**8. DOMINANT
SKILLFUL
SUPERIOR
FABULOUS
TALENTED
SPLENDID
SCHOOLED
EDUCATED
TERRIFIC
COMPLETE
MAJESTIC**

The ending "ful" means what you probably think it means -- "full of". SKILLFUL means "full of skill."

**9. MARVELOUS
FANTASTIC
UPLIFTING
BEAUTIFUL
UNEQUALED
MASTERFUL
WALLOPING**

WALLOPING comes from the word WALLOP, which means to hit very hard. A WALLOPING is a complete beating. If you lose a game by a score of 23 to 0, you took a walloping.

10. **STAGGERING**
    STUPENDOUS
    NOTEWORTHY
    CONSUMMATE
    TREMENDOUS

STAGGER means to walk unsteadily or wobbly. STAGGERING means so amazingly huge and impressive that you stagger when you see it.

CONSUMMATE comes from the Latin words "con", which means "with", and "summa", which means the greatest or highest.

11. **EXPERIENCED**
    UNSURPASSED
    OUTSTANDING
    EXCEPTIONAL
    MAGNIFICENT
    CRACKERJACK
    SUPERLATIVE
    ILLUSTRIOUS
    SENSATIONAL

CRACKERJACK is an easier way to say "crack jack." "Crack" means sharp or talented, and "jack" is a slang term for a man, so a CRACKERJACK is a talented person.

12. **ACCOMPLISHED**
    CONSIDERABLE
    MULTI-SKILLED
    ASTRONOMICAL
    UNPARALLELED
    PRIZEWINNING
    GREATHEARTED
    INCOMPARABLE

MULTI-SKILLED is a COMPOUND WORD, two words that are used together to mean something new. In this case, meaning having more than one skill.

13. **DISTINGUISHED**
    KNOWLEDGEABLE

A DISTINGUISHED person is noble, excellent, and probably has lots of knowledge (KNOWLEDGEABLE).

14. EXPRESSIVENESS

The ending "ness" means "having the quality of"

15. RESOURCEFULNESS

This has two endings, "ful" and "ness", so it has the quality of something that is full of resources.

16. ENTHUSIASTICALLY

Adding "ly" to the adjective ENTHUSIASTIC turns it into an ADVERB.

17. INDISTINGUISHABLE

The PREFIX "in", here, means "not" (it can mean inside or within in other words) and the SUFFIX "able" means "in the manner of" or "capable of", so this means not able to be distinguished.

18. PHENOMENOLOGICALLY

A PHENOMENON is something that happens that we can sense. The SUFFIX "logy" means science. PHENOMENOLOGY is the study of the universe as sensed by humans. Adding "ically" makes the word mean "like the study of sensed things."

19. STRAIGHTFORWARDNESS

For a long word, this one is pretty straightforward.

20. UNCHARACTERISTICALLY

Not like any defining feature of a person.

ALSO FROM H BAR PRESS

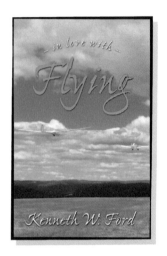

IN LOVE WITH FLYING

In this memoir, Kenneth Ford provides tales from his own years of flying light airplanes and gliders, and he profiles various aviators he has met along the way, people who impressed him with their passion for flying and who brought a special style to their love affair with flying.

This book is for anyone of any age who is thinking about becoming a pilot, or is already one, or who just appreciates the romance of the air. It's more than a collection of anecdotes. Ford is a teacher, and here you will learn, in non-technical language, about the kinds of lift that keep gliders aloft, the idiosyncrasies of "tail-dragger" airplanes, the art of landing in a crosswind, how pilots get from A to B, and more.

JANE

Jane was written and illustrated by Caroline Ford at the age of 12 when she was faced with having to store her dolls away. The book centers around the doll Jane, who is loved by Annie, then put away in a box until Annie grows up and has a daughter of her own to give Jane to.

ALSO FROM ADAM B. FORD

THE SIX SISTERS AND THEIR FLYING CARPETS

Six magical sisters clean the carpets in their big house by flying them joyfully around the town. Seeing this, the Prince of the province demands that the sisters teach him how to fly the carpets, but even though each sister teaches him a different way to fly them, the Prince never learns. He takes all the carpets to his palace, leaving the sisters with nothing but old blankets and bath mats, which the sisters fly with equal joy.

A great story for ages 6–10 of any gender, with a "strong and positive message in it, particularly for girls, but boys too, about trusting and having confidence in your own path and style, whatever it may be."

"This is a thoroughly charming tale about magic, trust, and perseverance." – Tilia Klebenov Jacobs, author, "Wrong Place Wrong Time"

h bar press

*729 Westview St.
Philadelphia, PA 19119
www.hbarpress.com*

All titles available from Amazon, Barnes & Noble, and through Ingram. Signed copies available by contacting the authors through hbarpress.com.

Thanks to Alex Dohan, Brad Bingham,
Ian Bruso, Eric Wernet, and Claire Hughes
for their stellar reviews.

ADAM FORD lives in East Wallingford, Vermont with his only-dog, Seera. He has written nine children's books, two screenplays, and three novels, and has a few more books in the works but gets lethargic and doesn't work on them as much as he should. He works in a sign shop but thinks that it might be time to do something else although he doesn't think that he could get paid to play ultimate, snowboard, or take artsy pictures. This is his second published work.

Adam likes funky hip-hop, but doesn't really recommend that readers of this book listen to Jurassic 5 until they get a little older.

COURTNEY HUDDLESTON lives somewhere in the mass of humid humanity that is Houston, Texas, where he is happily married to his wife and happily ball-and-chained to his art desk. Forever.

CPSIA information can be obtained
at www.ICGtesting.com
Printed in the USA
BVIC01n2152200813
329136BV00005B

* 9 7 8 0 9 7 9 4 1 0 4 9 9 *